Sea Dog

Dayle Campbell Gaetz

with illustrations by
Amy Meissner

ORCA BOOK PUBLISHERS

Library and Archives Canada Cataloguing in Publication

Gaetz, Dayle, 1947-

Sea dog / Dayle Campbell Gaetz; with illustrations by Amy Meissner.

(Orca echoes)

ISBN 1-55143-406-7

1. Dogs--Juvenile fiction. I. Meissner, Amy II. Title. III. Series.

PS8563.A25317S38 2006   jC813'.54   C2006-900339-4

First published in the United States 2006

Library of Congress Control Number: 2006920831

Summary: Kyle finds a dog washed up on the beach and claims it for his own;
when the dog's original owner shows up and tells his sad story, Kyle must make a hard choice.

Orca Book Publishers gratefully acknowledges the support for its publishing programs
provided by the following agencies: the Government of Canada through the Book
Publishing Industry Development Program and the Canada Council for the Arts, and the
Province of British Columbia through the BC Arts Council
and the Book Publishing Tax Credit.

Design by Lynn O'Rourke

Orca Book Publishers
PO Box 5626 Stn.B
Victoria, BC Canada
V8R 6S4

Orca Book Publishers
PO Box 468
Custer, WA USA
98240-0468

www.orcabook.com

Printed and bound in Canada.
Printed on 100% PCW recycled paper.

010 09 08 07 • 5 4 3 2

J. LOwry

for Jaime

Chapter One

Wind howled around Kyle's house. A big gust rattled his window. Rain pounded the roof above his head. Waves crashed on the beach.

Kyle pulled the covers over his head. He didn't want to think about his dad. But the storm made him remember. When there was a big storm, Dad always woke up early. He always made pancakes for breakfast.

He always called Kyle and Mom. They ate pancakes until they almost burst. While they ate they looked out the window. Waves tumbled and roared against the beach.

"This storm will bring lots of treasures," Dad always said.

After breakfast, Kyle and Dad always put on their rain slickers. They took their treasure bags. Hand in hand they went in search of treasure.

One day Dad found a glass fish float. Another time Kyle found a running shoe. It fit his left foot. The best treasure they ever found was a toy sailboat. It was yellow and red and had a white sail. "It must have fallen from someone's boat," Dad said.

That morning Kyle felt happy and sad. He felt happy for himself. He felt sad for the child who lost this special sailboat.

This morning Kyle felt sad again. He felt sad for himself. He pushed the covers from his face. Morning light crept around his window blinds. He looked at the beautiful toy boat on his dresser. His eyes watered.

There would be no more treasures. Dad didn't live here anymore.

Kyle shut his eyes tight. He tried not to think about treasures. He tried not to hear the roar of wind and waves. Soon he drifted off to sleep. He dreamed about Dad. He dreamed they walked along the beach hand in hand. He dreamed they found the other running shoe.

"Kyle!" his mom called.

Kyle's eyes flew open. He smelled coffee brewing. He smelled pancakes cooking. Was his dream real? He leapt out of bed and ran to the kitchen.

His mom was making pancakes. She bent to give him a big hug. "Go and get dressed," she said. "The wind is dying. It's almost time to search for treasures."

She smiled at him with watery eyes. Kyle blinked. His eyes filled with tears.

Mom and Kyle didn't eat very much. They weren't hungry today. They watched green and white waves break against the beach. Rain streaked down from a dark gray sky.

Kyle helped his mom clear the breakfast table. "Go put on your rain slicker," she said. "And don't forget your treasure bag."

Kyle didn't want to go out. But he didn't want to disappoint Mom. She was trying to make things better for him. So he dressed in his yellow rain slicker. He took his red mesh treasure bag from its hook.

They walked hand in hand along the sand. Clumps of seaweed lay tangled on the shore. Chunks of driftwood dotted the beach. Kyle carried his treasure bag and tried to smile.

"Look, Kyle." His mom stopped at a clump of seaweed. "This might hold a treasure."

Kyle lifted handfuls of green eelgrass. He dragged a long brown piece of kelp from the clump. It felt cold and slimy in his bare hands. Underneath was a stick of driftwood. "Not much of a treasure," he said.

The stick was just right for walking, though. Kyle carried it with him. He poked at another clump of seaweed. Underneath was a big, red, dead jellyfish.

"Don't touch," Mom said. "The stingers hurt even after the jellyfish dies."

"That's no treasure." Kyle sighed. He wanted to go home.

"Look at that!" Mom said.

Kyle looked down the beach, near the water's edge. He saw a huge clump of tangled seaweed.

"I'll bet there's a treasure under there," Mom said. They lifted away handfuls of seaweed. They moved chunks of driftwood. Underneath was a huge, flat driftwood board. On it lay something black. And wet. And hairy. It was tangled in seaweed.

"Don't touch," Mom said. "I think it's a dead seal."

But Kyle lifted one more handful of seaweed. "It has an ear," he said. "It looks like a dog."

"Poor dog," Mom said. "It must have drowned in the storm last night."

Kyle pulled away more seaweed. He uncovered the dog's face. "Its eyelid moved! It's alive!"

Chapter Two

They uncovered the rest of the dog. It lay still on its driftwood board.

Mom put her hand on the dog's chest. "It's breathing!" she said.

"We need to take it home," Kyle said. "How can we carry it?"

Mom took off her rain slicker and covered the dog. "You stay here," she said. "I have an idea."

Kyle sat on the wet sand beside the wet dog. He patted the dog's head and scratched behind its ear. "Please live," he whispered. "I promise to take good care of you."

Mom returned with the wheelbarrow. It was lined with towels and covered with a tarp. "Kyle," she said, "you lift the dog's head. I'll lift its body. We'll put it in the wheelbarrow."

The soggy dog lay limp in their arms. They laid it on the dry towels. They placed the tarp over top. Kyle put his stick and his bag in the wheelbarrow. He helped push the heavy wheelbarrow across the soft, wet sand.

They carried the dripping dog into the house. They laid her beside the woodstove. Kyle got some fresh towels. He rubbed the dog all over. The dog coughed, and water trickled from her mouth. She shivered.

"I'm going to phone the vet," Mom said.

Kyle sat close beside the dog. He stroked her head. "Please don't die," he whispered.

Mom returned. "The vet said to warm some towels in the dryer," she said. Kyle helped wrap warm towels around the cold dog.

"She said to put a hot water bottle near her chest," Mom said. So that's what they did.

"You stay with the dog. I'm going to heat some milk."

"Did the vet say that too?"

Mom nodded.

Mom brought warm milk in a bowl. She put it near the dog's nose. The dog half opened her eyes. Her pink tongue hung out, but she didn't drink.

"I have an idea," Kyle said. He went to the kitchen for the turkey baster. He dipped it into the warm milk. He pumped the bulb until milk rose into the tube. He dropped warm milk on the dog's pink tongue. She licked.

Kyle dropped more milk onto her tongue. She licked some more. Then she lifted her head and lapped up all the milk. Her head flopped back down. She curled up in her warm towels. She lay close to the warm woodstove. Soon she fell asleep.

Kyle sat beside her and watched her breathe.

"I think she'll be all right," Mom said. "Shall we give her a name?"

Kyle nodded. "Let's call her Treasure. She's the best treasure we ever found."

All that rainy morning Kyle sat beside Treasure. At lunchtime Mom reheated the pancakes. They ate every bite. Treasure drank some more warm milk.

After lunch Mom and Kyle went out. They needed to buy dog food and a dog dish. Treasure slept by the woodstove. When they came back, Treasure sat up and wagged her tail. "She's happy to see us!" Kyle said.

He put dog food into the shiny new dish. Treasure gobbled it up. Then she curled up and went back to sleep.

"How come she sleeps so much?" Kyle asked.

"She might be sick or she might be very old," Mom said. "Or she might just be tired."

"I think she's tired," Kyle said.

Treasure slept all afternoon and all night long.

Chapter Three

Early the next morning Kyle opened his eyes. Two brown eyes stared back at him. "Treasure!" he cried. "You're better!"

Treasure licked Kyle's nose. Her tongue felt warm and sticky.

Outside, sun sparkled on a rippled sea. "Let's walk along the beach," Kyle said after breakfast.

Kyle took his walking stick from the wheelbarrow. Treasure sat and barked at it. He gave the stick to Treasure and she ran away. She bounded into the water. Kyle ran to the water's edge. By then Treasure was a long way from shore.

"Treasure!" he called. "Come back!"

A lone white boat sailed far out on the rippled sea. Treasure's nose pointed toward it. But the boat sailed farther and farther away.

Kyle ran into the water. It was cold on his legs. "Treasure!" he called.

At last Treasure turned around and swam back. She still had the stick in her mouth.

After that Kyle hurried home from school every day. He always took Treasure for a walk along the beach. She always carried the same stick. She always went swimming. But she never swam so far from shore again.

Sometimes Kyle went out with his dad, but it wasn't the same. When Kyle came home, he always felt sad. He always took Treasure for a walk on the beach. She helped him feel less lonely.

Spring came and the days grew longer. One warm sunny afternoon, Kyle took Treasure for a walk. For once she didn't run into the water. Instead, she streaked along the beach. She still carried her stick in her mouth.

"Treasure, come back!" Kyle called. But the dog paid no attention.

She ran along the sandbar and Kyle ran after her. He saw Treasure leaping around a tall man. The man carried a pipe in his mouth. He had a big gray beard.

Treasure dropped her stick. She leaped up and down and quivered with excitement.

The man took his pipe from his mouth. He crouched down and put his arms around the dog. Treasure licked his face.

"By gum, it's you, Otter! I can't believe it! You ought-ter be drowned!"

The man looked at Kyle. There were tears in his eyes. "Thank you for finding my dog," he said.

Chapter Four

Kyle looked at the man. He felt scared and angry. This man wanted to take Treasure away.

"Her name's Treasure, not Otter! And she's my dog, not yours!"

"Kyle!" his mom called. She ran toward them.

Kyle watched his mom and tried not to cry.

"Is there a problem here?" she asked.

"That man says Treasure is his dog!" Kyle pointed at the man.

"Hi," the man said. He smiled. "I'm Bill. I'm so happy to see my dog again. She fell overboard in a big storm. I searched for a long, long time. Finally I gave up. I thought she had drowned."

"She's my Treasure!" Kyle shouted. "I found her on the beach. She was all wrapped up in seaweed."

Bill smiled again. "That's my Otter. She's a great old sea dog."

"She's my dog!" Kyle shouted. "Here Treasure!" Treasure licked Kyle's face.

Bill stopped smiling. "I'd say we have a problem here."

"Please, come back to our house," Mom said. "I'll make coffee and we can talk."

Kyle didn't want to talk to Bill. Bill was not a nice man. He wanted to take Treasure away. Treasure picked up her stick. She walked between Kyle and Bill. Her tail wagged all the way back to the house.

Mom and Bill sat in the kitchen. Kyle took Treasure into his room. He packed some clothes in his schoolbag. "Shh!" he whispered. "We're going to find my dad. He'll let me keep you."

They tiptoed to the front door. Bill's voice drifted down the hall. Kyle heard two words, "*Lady Tia.*"

Treasure stopped. Her ears perked up. She turned and ran to the kitchen.

Bill laughed. "You love the *Lady Tia,* don't you, Otter?"

Kyle moved close to the kitchen door. He waited for Treasure to come back.

Bill sighed. "My boat is for sale," he said. "I didn't feel like sailing after I lost Otter. I missed her too much."

"Why did you name her Otter?" Mom asked.

Bill chuckled. "Because she swims like an otter. She's the best sea dog that ever lived."

"Tell us about her," Mom said.

Kyle crept into the kitchen. He leaned on a wall and sank to the floor. He pulled his knees to his chest and stared straight ahead. He didn't want to hear Bill's story. But he couldn't leave without Treasure.

Bill leaned back on his chair. He rubbed a hand over his big gray beard. Then he started to talk.

Chapter Five

First I will tell you about my daughter, Tia.

When Tia was seven, I bought a beautiful sailboat. I named it *Lady Tia*. When we were on the sailboat, Tia always called me Cap'n Bill. We were happy sailing together.

Year after year, Tia grew. She grew bigger and older. The time came when she needed to move far away.

Before she left, she came to say good-bye. We sat on the deck of *Lady Tia*.

"I have a special gift for you," she said. In her arms was a tiny, wiggly, black bundle.

"What is it?" I asked.

"This is a very special puppy. She was born on a boat, and she loves the sea."

Well, I didn't want a puppy. But I didn't want to disappoint Tia. She was trying to make things better for me.

"Thank you," I said.

"Good-bye, Cap'n Bill." Tia gave me a big hug. "I'll always miss sailing with you." Then she went away.

The puppy wiggled in my arms. I almost dropped her overboard. So I took her down the ladder. I put her on a bunk inside the *Lady Tia*.

I climbed back up the ladder. I sat on deck and puffed on my pipe. The wind blew at my back. I smelled the crisp salty air. Outside the harbor, choppy waves called to me. *Come sail with us! Come sail with us!*

I didn't want to hear.

Lady Tia was sparkly clean. Her sails were ready to raise. But I didn't feel like sailing. "Well old girl,"

I rubbed my hand along her shiny wood trim, "I reckon it's time I sold you."

Lady Tia shuddered in the wind. Her lines clattered fast and hard against the mast. *Clang-clang-clang-clang*. I always loved that sound. It made me want to untie *Lady Tia*. It made me long to sail a windswept sea.

I loved the creak and groan of the rigging.

I loved the way *Lady Tia* sliced through the waves. She sailed faster than the wind blew.

I loved the soft cool touch of salt spray on my face.

But not that day. That day I sat on deck and puffed on my pipe. I listened to waves slap, slap, slapping against the clean white hull. I looked out the narrow gap that led to the sea. I saw green and white waves tumble and splash.

"It's a perfect day to sail," I said. But I didn't get up. I didn't untie the ropes that held *Lady Tia* fast.

Then something caught my eye. A black speck

rose to the crest of a wave. It swam like an otter. Then it was gone.

I saw it again, on the next wave. "It's too small for a seal," I said, "but too black for an otter." There was no one to hear me. Maybe I was talking to *Lady Tia*. Maybe I was talking to myself.

I put down my pipe. Green and white waves tumbled and splashed. The black speck was hard to find. It rose and fell with every wave. Wind and tide pushed it away. Soon I could barely see it.

Then I had a terrible thought. I leaped from my seat. I ran down the ladder. The puppy was not in the cabin. I ran back outside. I stepped to the dock.

"How did she get out there?" I untied the bow rope.

"She won't last much longer." I untied the stern rope.

"It's all my fault." I pushed the bow out from the dock.

"I need to save her." I stepped on board.

Chapter Six

I pulled the line to raise the mainsail. That big white sail rose up, up. It rose to the top of the mast.

Wind filled the sail. It puffed out like a white balloon. *Lady Tia* leaped forward. She danced over the waves. Water gurgled behind her stern. A little trail of dimples followed behind us.

I set the sail and turned the tiller. *Lady Tia* turned her nose to the sea.

Lady Tia slipped through the gap into the open sea. Her bow dipped and rolled. Waves splashed over her side. I held the tiller steady and searched the choppy water. Waves broke into white foam. Chunks of driftwood bobbed up and down.

Seaweed tangled together. But the little black speck was nowhere to be seen.

I felt worse than lonely. I felt terrible. "Poor little pup," I whispered. "She must be lonely. Maybe she's looking for her mother. I should never have left her all alone. She must have climbed the ladder. She must have fallen overboard. I didn't even hear a splash."

I turned *Lady Tia's* nose into the wind. Her mainsail flapped. *Lady Tia* stood dead in the water.

I stood up and searched the white-flecked sea. "Nothing but driftwood and seaweed pulled loose by the storm. No sign of a little black puppy." I knew she must be tired. She would not last long in that cold water.

The sea looked empty. Lonely and empty and sad. But I couldn't give up. I fixed the tiller in place. Then I crept over the deck to the mast. I pulled the line to raise the jib sail. The jib rose up and up. It flapped in the wind.

I crept back to the tiller. I pulled the lines to make both sails puff out. *Crash!* The boom swung over my head. *Lady Tia* bounded over the waves like a deer in a meadow.

I sat down to steer *Lady Tia* in a big circle. As I steered I searched the waves for a tiny black speck. But I didn't hold out much hope. Too much time had passed.

Chunks of driftwood bobbed up and down. Seaweed tangled together. Cold salt spray tickled my face. Water gurgled around *Lady Tia*. The rigging creaked and groaned.

And yipped.

"Now, *Lady Tia,* there's a sound you never made before," I said.

Yip!

The *yip* was weak, but my ears were good. I knew it did not come from *Lady Tia*.

It came from the sea. I studied the tangled seaweed. I looked at the driftwood. Some pieces were as small as a twig. Some were as big as a tree. One piece was wide and flat. It floated low in the water. Long brown kelp and thin green eelgrass covered it. The seaweed moved ever so slightly.

"Aha!" I cried. "Now, aren't you a smart little pup?"

I turned *Lady Tia* into the wind. She stopped dead in the water. The flat chunk of driftwood floated closer.

I leaned over the side.

Chapter Seven

I leaned over so far my fingers touched the water. I leaned so far I almost fell overboard.

The driftwood bumped against *Lady Tia's* shiny white hull. It bobbed up and down. It drifted close to my hands. "A-ha!" I scooped it out of the water.

It was a huge clump of dripping wet seaweed. I laid it on deck and lifted handfuls of seaweed. I tossed the seaweed overboard. Underneath was a wide flat board. On the board was a very tiny, very wet puppy.

The puppy's eyes were closed tight. The tip of her little pink tongue hung out from her mouth. The puppy didn't move.

"Oh, Puppy," I said. "I am so sorry. I should never have left you alone. I should never have let you fall overboard."

Very gently I picked up the puppy. I put her on my lap and rubbed her tummy. Water trickled from her mouth. She shivered.

This was a good sign and a bad sign. It meant the pup was still alive, but she was very cold. I needed to warm her quickly. So I took off my wool sweater. I rubbed the pup all over. Then I tucked her inside my shirt. She snuggled against my stomach.

"Ugh!" I said to the cold wet pup. "You are as cold as the sea."

I was cold too. So I put on my damp wool sweater. I turned *Lady Tia* around.

"Please live," I whispered to the pup. "I'll take you home and warm you up." The pup snuggled close, wet and cold and shivering.

As soon as I tied up *Lady Tia,* I started along the dock. With both hands I clutched that cold little

lump against my stomach. "We're almost back to my car," I whispered. "I'll turn on the heater, and you'll soon be warm."

A woman on the dock gave me a strange look. "Hey, Cap'n Bill," she said. "Why are you talking to your stomach?"

"I need to hurry home," I told her.

I walked across the parking lot. My sweater was wet. I smelled like seaweed.

"We're here," I whispered.

A man in the parking lot gave me a strange look. "Hey, Cap'n Bill," he said. "Why is your stomach moving?"

"I need to hurry home," I told him.

On the way home that little wet bundle lay very still. "Please live," I whispered. "I promise to take good care of you."

At home I lifted my sweater. I untucked my shirt. I pulled out a little black bundle.

The pup shivered.

I phoned the vet. She told me what to do.

I laid the pup on a hot water bottle. I wrapped warm towels around her. I held her on my lap. Then I heard a strange sound. "Is that your rumbly tummy?"

I warmed some milk, but she wouldn't drink. Then I had an idea.

I carried the pup to the house next door. A big family lives there.

"Hi, Bill," the mother said.

"Do you have a baby bottle?" I asked.

"What a cute little pup!" she said. "Does it have a name?"

I thought for a minute. "I think I'll call her Otter. Because she ought-ter have drowned."

Otter liked the baby bottle. She sucked and swallowed, sucked and swallowed. She drank all the milk. Then she yawned and went to sleep.

That night Otter curled up on my bed. She slept under my blanket. Warm and safe.

Chapter Eight

For two days Otter slept most of the time. On the third day she woke up bursting with energy. She wrestled with my hand. She chewed on my fingers with her little puppy teeth. She ran around in circles. Round and round and round.

The next day I took her to the beach.

Otter ran straight for the water. She splashed into the cold sea. She started to swim away. "Otter!" I called. "Come back here!"

Otter turned around. She swam and ducked underwater. At last she swam back to shore. I scooped her up. "Otter is a good name for you," I said. "You swim like an otter."

Otter grew. She drank milk and grew plump.

She ate puppy food and grew bigger. Every time I took her to the beach she went swimming.

One day we went to a pet store. I bought a bright orange life jacket. Then I bought a cardboard sign and a black felt pen.

I carried Otter along the dock. *Lady Tia* bobbed gently at her mooring. I stepped aboard. I tied one end of a rope to Otter's life jacket. I tied the other end to a cleat on *Lady Tia's* deck. "That will keep you safe," I said. I sat the chubby puppy on a seat.

I picked up the sign. I wrote my phone number on it. I taped the sign to *Lady Tia's* window. The sign said: FOR SALE.

A sea wind ruffled my hair. The smell of salt water tickled my nostrils. My heart felt heavy. I would miss *Lady Tia*. I looked at the seat where Otter ought-ter be. My heart did a flip-flop. She was gone!

"Otter!" I cried. Then I remembered the rope. It snaked along the seat. It climbed up to the deck above the cabin. It trailed across the deck to the mast.

A tiny black tail, no bigger than my finger, poked out behind the mast. It wagged as fast as a hummingbird's wing.

I climbed up to the mast. I looked down at the pup. Her little black nose pointed toward the sea. Salty wind blew her ears back. Her mouth opened in a puppy-smile. Her little body shook with excitement.

"So you want to go sailing, do you, Otter?" I asked. "Well, I guess it won't hurt. We'll take *Lady Tia* on one last sail. But mind you don't fall overboard. If you do, you'll never get near a boat again."

Otter sat on the seat. She watched me untie the boat. She watched *Lady Tia* slide through the gap. Her little pink tongue hung out. She watched the sails go up. Her head twisted to one side.

Wind filled the sails. *Lady Tia* heeled to one side. Water gurgled behind her stern. *Lady Tia* pranced into the waves.

A warm little body snuggled up beside me. Otter

sat up straight, her nose pointed into the wind. I patted the top of her head. Her tail wagged.

"You're a real little sea dog," I said.

Soft sea spray touched my cheeks. Green and white waves tumbled over one another. I smiled as we headed out to sea.

That evening the wind dropped to a gentle breeze. The waves smoothed into a rippled sea. I steered *Lady Tia* toward the harbor.

Otter watched me light my pipe. Her head turned to one side. She watched me clutch it between my teeth. Her little pink tongue hung out.

She jumped to the floor. She sniffed at a stick of driftwood. It had been there since I pulled Otter from the sea. She picked up the stick. She climbed back up to the seat. She sat close beside me.

Otter chewed on her stick. I puffed on my pipe. *Lady Tia* sailed gently with the wind.

When we got back to the marina I took the For Sale sign down.

Chapter Nine

All summer long Otter grew. All summer long we sailed together.

In fall the days grew shorter. The winds blew stronger. Still we sailed together. Still Otter grew.

Winter came, and it was too cold to sail. I had *Lady Tia* hauled from the water. I covered her with tarps. They would protect her from winter storms.

I stood in my yard and looked at *Lady Tia*. "We will sail you again in spring," I said.

I walked to my back door. Otter walked beside me. I puffed on my pipe. Otter carried her stick.

I put down my pipe on the porch. Otter put down her stick. We went inside the warm house.

"Next spring I will be Cap'n Bill again," I said. "But now I am just plain Bill."

Every day Otter and I went for a walk. Sometimes we walked along a beach. Sometimes we walked through the woods. Wherever we went, I took my pipe. Otter always carried a stick. The bigger she grew, the bigger the stick.

Even when rain pounded down from thick dark clouds... Even when strong cold winds stormed across the sea... Even when waves crashed against the shore... Even on those days, Otter wanted to swim. She always dropped her stick at my feet.

"It's too cold to swim today," I always said. I walked past the stick. Otter picked it up. She ran ahead of me. She dropped it at my feet again. She looked up and barked.

I laughed and tossed the stick into the water. Otter bounded after it. Her black head bobbed on the waves. Sometimes she disappeared. Then I saw her again. She rolled to the top of a wave.

One day a big black seal heard Otter bark. It swam up close. It lifted high in the water. Its big round eyes stared at this strange animal. This animal chased a stick instead of a fish.

The seal followed Otter toward shore. It blinked and watched this strange animal. This animal ran from the water. It had long thin legs instead of flippers.

Otter ran to drop the stick at my feet. She shook her thick black coat. Cold water sprayed all over me.

"Go away!" I shouted. "That's freezing!"

Otter picked up her stick and ran along the beach.

Spring came again. The days grew longer. The wind that stirred the sea grew warmer.

Otter sat in the yard. She watched me scrape and paint and polish. She chewed on her stick and wagged her tail. Soon we would be sailing again.

At last *Lady Tia* was sparkly clean and ready to sail. I had her hauled back to the harbor.

I stepped onto *Lady Tia's* deck. Otter jumped aboard. "It feels good to be Cap'n Bill again," I said. Otter wagged her tail.

I picked up Otter's life jacket. I tried to put it on her, but it was too small. "Maybe you don't need a life jacket anymore," I said. "You swim like an otter, and you never fall overboard."

Otter wagged her tail.

We sailed on brisk spring winds. *Lady Tia* heeled over and danced across the waves. Her rigging creaked and groaned. Otter sat on the seat beside me. Cool sea spray washed over our faces.

The summer winds were light and warm. On hot days I anchored *Lady Tia* in a bay. I climbed into my dinghy and rowed to shore.

Otter jumped from *Lady Tia's* deck. She landed with a splash in the water. She swam to shore with strong sure strokes. "You're a real sea dog," I said. "You love to swim so much."

Sometimes we slept all night on the boat. I lay on the forward berth. Otter curled up beside me. I left my pipe in an ashtray outside. Otter left her stick on the seat beside it.

Chapter Ten

That long summer came to an end. The days grew shorter. It was almost time to have *Lady Tia* hauled from the water.

One morning I woke up and looked out the window. Sun shone from a bright blue sky. Cedar trees swayed on a gentle breeze. "Let's go for one last sail before winter," I said.

Otter barked and wagged her tail.

I packed sandwiches and coffee for myself. I packed dog biscuits for Otter. And off we went.

The west wind blew steadily. *Lady Tia* pranced into the wind. At noon I ate my sandwiches and drank my coffee. Otter gobbled her dog biscuits. She drank water from her dish.

By late afternoon the wind blew stronger. It switched to the southeast. Dark clouds rose over the islands. "It's time to head home," I said.

I turned *Lady Tia* around. A strong wind billowed her sails. *Lady Tia* heeled over. She picked up speed. Water gurgled around her hull. Wind snapped at her sails.

"I don't like the look of this," I said. I reefed in the mainsail to make it smaller. "That's better," I told Otter. "We need less sail in this strong wind."

Soon the wind blew even stronger. *Lady Tia* heeled farther over. Her bow dipped into the waves. Seawater poured onto her deck.

I fixed the tiller in place.

Otter sat on the seat. She clutched her special stick. I patted her head. "You sit tight," I told her. "I need to change the jib."

I made my way along the deck. *Lady Tia* bucked and rolled beneath my feet. Water sloshed around my sea boots. If I didn't hang on tight I would fall overboard. I lowered the jib sail. I put up a small storm jib. "That's better," I said.

I made my way back to the seat. *Lady Tia* bucked and rolled. *Crash!* The boom swung over my head.

When I got back the seat was empty.

"Otter!" I called. There was no answer.

I looked inside the cabin. Otter wasn't there.

"Oh, no!" I cried. I looked across the sea. Green and white waves tumbled and rolled. Clumps of seaweed rose and fell. Chunks of driftwood bobbed on rolling waves. Then I spotted a dark head. My heart lightened. "Otter!" I called.

The head turned. Two round eyes blinked at me. The head was round and smooth. It had no ears. "Where's Otter?" I yelled. The seal sank beneath the waves.

I turned *Lady Tia* around. I searched until the

sun sank behind the islands. I searched until the sea turned black as ink. Tears stung my eyes. "I should have bought her a new life jacket."

At last I turned *Lady Tia's* bow toward home.

My heart ached.

Chapter Eleven

"So, that's my story," Bill sighed "That's how I lost Otter. I thought she had drowned."

He sipped his coffee and stared at his hands.

Kyle got up from the kitchen floor. He sat on a chair beside his mom. There was something wet on Bill's cheek.

Bill wiped it away. "I put a FOR SALE sign on *Lady Tia*," he said. "It's time I sold her. First I sailed with Tia, but she moved away. Then I sailed with Otter, but she fell overboard. I don't feel like sailing any more."

Bill smiled, but his smile went all wobbly. "I am very happy you found her, Kyle. You saved Otter's life. And now I see that you love her too. I will not take her away. That would be wrong."

Kyle tried to feel happy. He tried to smile, but his smile went wobbly too. He felt so sad he wanted to cry. But the sadness was not for himself. It was for Bill.

Bill lived all alone. Kyle lived with his mom.

Bill's daughter moved far away. Kyle's dad lived close by.

Bill didn't see Tia very often. Kyle saw his dad every week.

Kyle looked at his mom. She smiled at him. She didn't say a word.

Kyle looked at Treasure. The dog put her nose on his knee. He patted her head.

Bill stood up. "Thank you for the coffee," he said. He bent to pat the dog. "Good-bye, Treasure," he said. He walked slowly to the door.

"You take her!" Kyle called. "You take Otter. You need her more than me!"

Bill turned around. "Oh!" he said.

He smiled a real smile this time. The dog ran to him. He bent to scratch behind her ear. "Thank you, Kyle."

Kyle tried to feel happy. But his eyes stung. His heart ached.

Bill looked at Kyle. "I have a better idea," he said. "You love this dog as much as I do. Why don't we share her? I'll take her sailing when you're at school. You can pick her up on your way home."

Kyle ran over. He scratched behind the dog's other ear. "Okay." He smiled at Bill, a huge happy smile.

"Well," Bill said. "I must go now. I want to take the For Sale sign down." He walked to the door again. "I feel like sailing after all."

Kyle grinned. "I'm seven, but I've never ever been sailing!"

Bill turned around. He looked at Mom. She smiled and nodded.

"Then some days the three of us will sail together. You, me and Treasure."

"But, you said her name is Otter!"

"On the boat I am no longer Bill. I am Cap'n Bill. When we are sailing the dog will be Otter. The rest of the time we'll call her Treasure. That's a better name anyway, don't you think?"

Kyle looked at Bill. He nodded. "She's the best treasure anyone ever found!"

Dayle Campbell Gaetz is the author of several books for children and teens. She lives in Campbell River, British Columbia.